Think Green! Think Green!

Sally Huss

ISBN: 0692676716
ISBN 13: 9780692676714

"Think Green! Think Green!"

That's what it said on the truck that I was seeing.

I asked, "What does it mean to 'Think Green?'"

"Ah," said my mother, who is wiser than me,

"To think green is an absolute necessity.

It means to keep things clean like the color green

Which can be found

In nearly everything that comes from the ground."

"The grass is green," I had to agree,

"And so is every plant and the top of every tree."

"Yes," she said, as we got out of the car.

I threw off the paper from my ice cream bar.

"No! No!" my mother chided. "Pick up the wrapper.

We don't want to leave a scrap of trash here."

To please her, I put it in the trashcan.

"We're all working," she said, "on a new plan –

To keep our earth clean.

Think green! Think green!"

As I put the wrapper in the can,

I too felt that I was part of this plan.

"What else," I asked, "do we need to keep clean?"

"The oceans and streams. These need to be kept clean."

This is what she said,

As we walked toward the beach ahead.

I asked, "Why do we need to keep the ocean clean?"

"For all the fish and animals that live in it that cannot be seen.

They breathe water instead of air,

So it is important that we take good care."

With that, I picked up a plastic bag

from the sand and a soda can.

I was feeling more and more like I was part of the plan.

As I looked at all the people along the beach,

With their baskets and umbrellas,

as far as my eye could reach…

I could see that some were tidy and seemed to care.

Others were definitely not so aware.

They left messes for others to clean.

They didn't know the importance of thinking green.

Our trip to the beach

Was an opportunity for my mother to teach.

But that was not the only place for me to learn something new.

We stopped at the market to pick up some things for a stew.

There, right there in the vegetable aisle,

My mother waved her hand with great style,

"Even with food, we should be thinking green.

All the green foods keep our bodies healthy and clean…

Especially those marked 'ORGANIC.'

They have not been sprayed and are considered non-toxic."

"What about the colorful fruits?" I wanted to know.

"Oh!" she said, "They are the ones that give us that glow.

They have natural sugars that keep us bright.

We'll take a few home to have for dessert tonight."

On the way home I pressed my nose to the glass,

Looking for more opportunities to think green as we passed.

I said to my mother, "What about all the fumes from that truck?

Isn't it filling the air with gaseous muck?"

"Yes," said my mother with a knowing sigh.

"One day we'll take better care of our beautiful blue sky."

At home, after a delicious and healthy dinner,

I helped my mother make the table cleaner.

Then I helped my father take out the trash –

Some was for recycling, some was just garbagy trash.

There again were those words: "Think Green! Think Green!"

Now I knew what they really did mean.

It was off to a bath with a tub full of bubbles,

Each one cleaning my skin from the day's sand and rubbles.

The toothpaste did the same for my teeth and gums.

I liked this greenness; it was really quite fun.

Before I went to sleep that night

My mother came in to say goodnight.

She said, "There is another area to keep clean,

Another area in which to think green.

Any unhappy thoughts or feelings that have bothered you today

You can now let them float away.

If you kiss them goodbye you will make your inner self clean

And be ready for a night filled with a wonderful dream.

By doing this, you will prepare the way

To make tomorrow a perfect day."

So, I said goodbye to any sadness or unpleasantness that I had felt

And off to dreamland I seemed to melt.

Yes, just as my mother had promised me

My tomorrow arrived most happily.

The end,
but not the end
of caring for
our planet earth.

At the end of this book you will find a Certificate of Merit that may be issued to any child who has fulfilled the requirements stated in the Certificate. This fine Certificate will easily fit into a 5"x7" frame, and happily suit any girl or boy who receives it!

Sally writes new books all the time. If you would like to be alerted when one of her new books becomes available or when one of her books is offered FREE on Amazon, sign up here: http://www.sallyhuss.com/kids-books.html.

If you liked *Think Green! Think Green!* please be kind enough to post a short review on Amazon. Here is the link: http://amzn.to/1Pop8Xa.

Here are a few Sally Huss books you might enjoy. They may be found on Amazon as e-books or in soft cover.

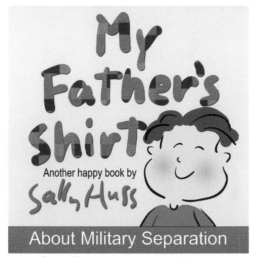

http://amzn.com/B018JQP8S0

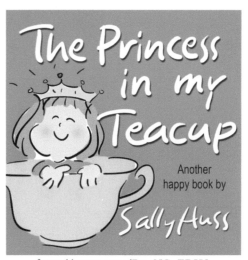

http://amzn.com/B00NG4EDH8

http://amzn.com/B0125714B4

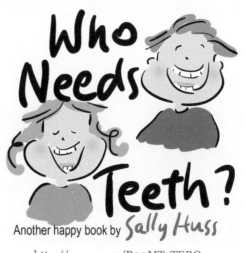

http://amzn.com/B00MT5TER0

About the Author/Illustrator

Sally Huss

"Bright and happy," "light and whimsical" have been the catch phrases attached to the writings and art of Sally Huss for over 30 years. Sweet images dance across all of Sally's creations, whether in the form of children's books, paintings, wallpaper, ceramics, baby bibs, purses, clothing, or her King Features syndicated newspaper panel "Happy Musings."

Sally creates children's books to uplift the lives of children and hopes you will join her in this effort by helping spread her happy messages.

Sally is a graduate of USC with a degree in Fine Art and through the years has had 26 of her own licensed art galleries throughout the world.

This certificate may be cut out, framed, and presented to any child who has earned it.

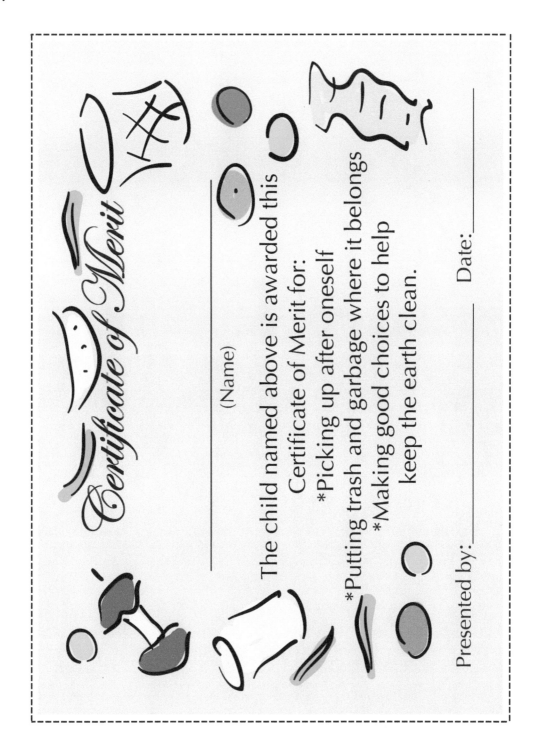

Certificate of Merit

_____
(Name)

The child named above is awarded this Certificate of Merit for:
*Picking up after oneself
*Putting trash and garbage where it belongs
*Making good choices to help keep the earth clean.

Presented by: _____

Date: _____

CPSIA information can be obtained
at www.ICGtesting.com
Printed in the USA
BVHW021817150821
614473BV000l0B/43